The Yawn That Went 'Round the World

By Gene Mandarino

TIGER STRIPE PUBLISHING

CHICAGO

Published by

Tiger Stripe Publishing
Chicago, IL
TigerStripePub.com

Names: Mandarino, Gene.

Title: Yawn! The Yawn That Went 'Round the World / by Gene Mandarino.
Description: Chicago, IL: Tiger Stripe Publishing, 2018. | Summary: When bedtime draws near and the moon begins to yawn, children and animals pick up the contagious yawn until it gently goes around the world.

Identifiers: ISBN 978-0-9905895-9-4
Subjects: LCSH: Bedtime – Juvenile Fiction. | Stories in rhyme. | Yawning–Juvenile fiction. | BISAC: JUVENILE FICTION / Bedtime & Dreams.

Classification: LCC PZ7 | DDC [E] –dc23

23 22 21 20 19 18   1 2 3 4 5

First printing in the United States, January 2018

To Ed Klann, Harry Cortesman, and Bob Fryml. The wisdom you passed on to me opened my world.

Thanks forever

There is something magic in a yawn,

the moon said with a sigh.

When you see one coming,

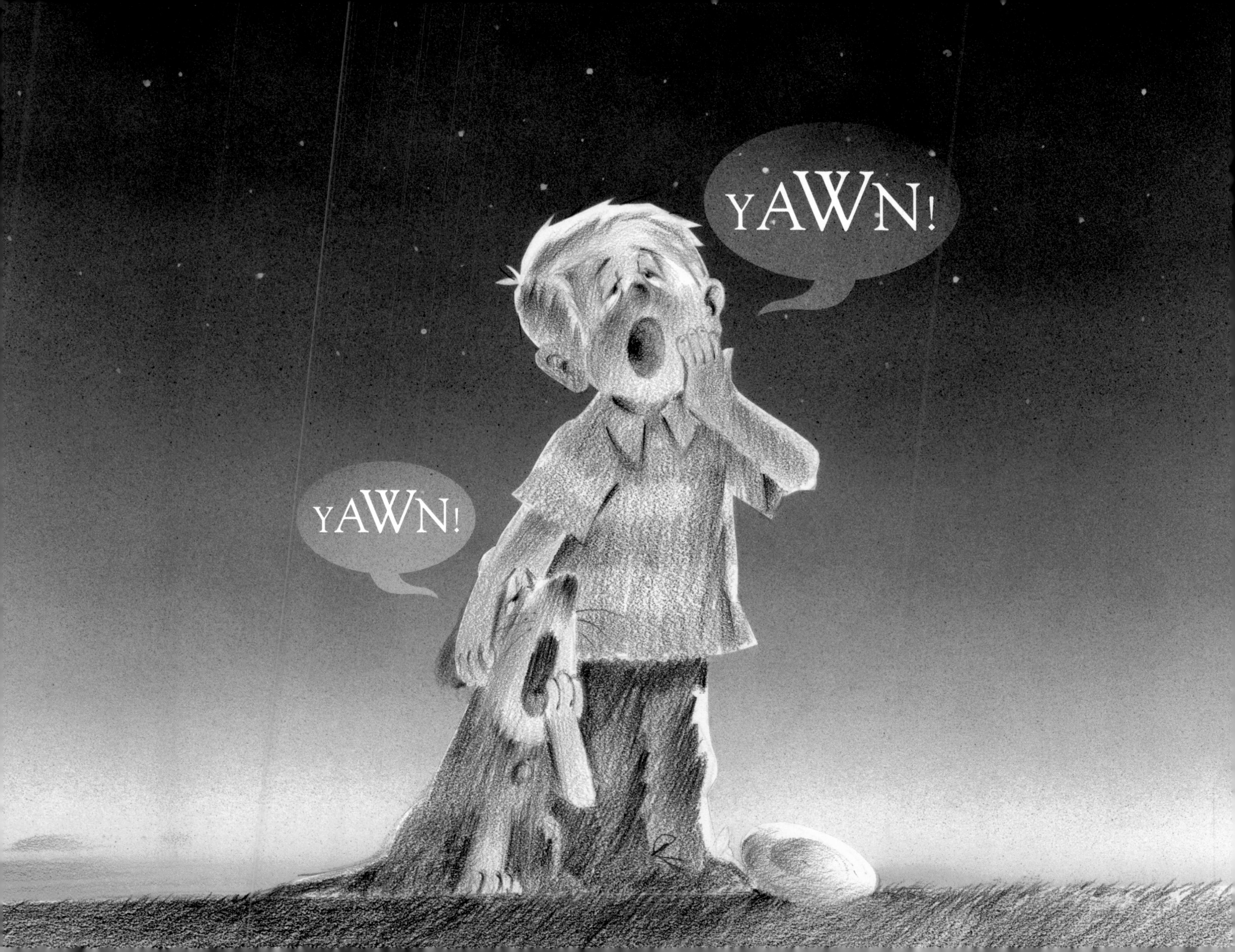
YAWN!
YAWN!

you'll know it's beddy-bye.

It can take your worries and troubles of the day,

and with one big wide yawn,

they all will drift away.

So when you see one coming,
you'll know just what to do.

Goodness gracious. It's contagious!
You'll have to do one, too!

So pass one on to Jasmine,

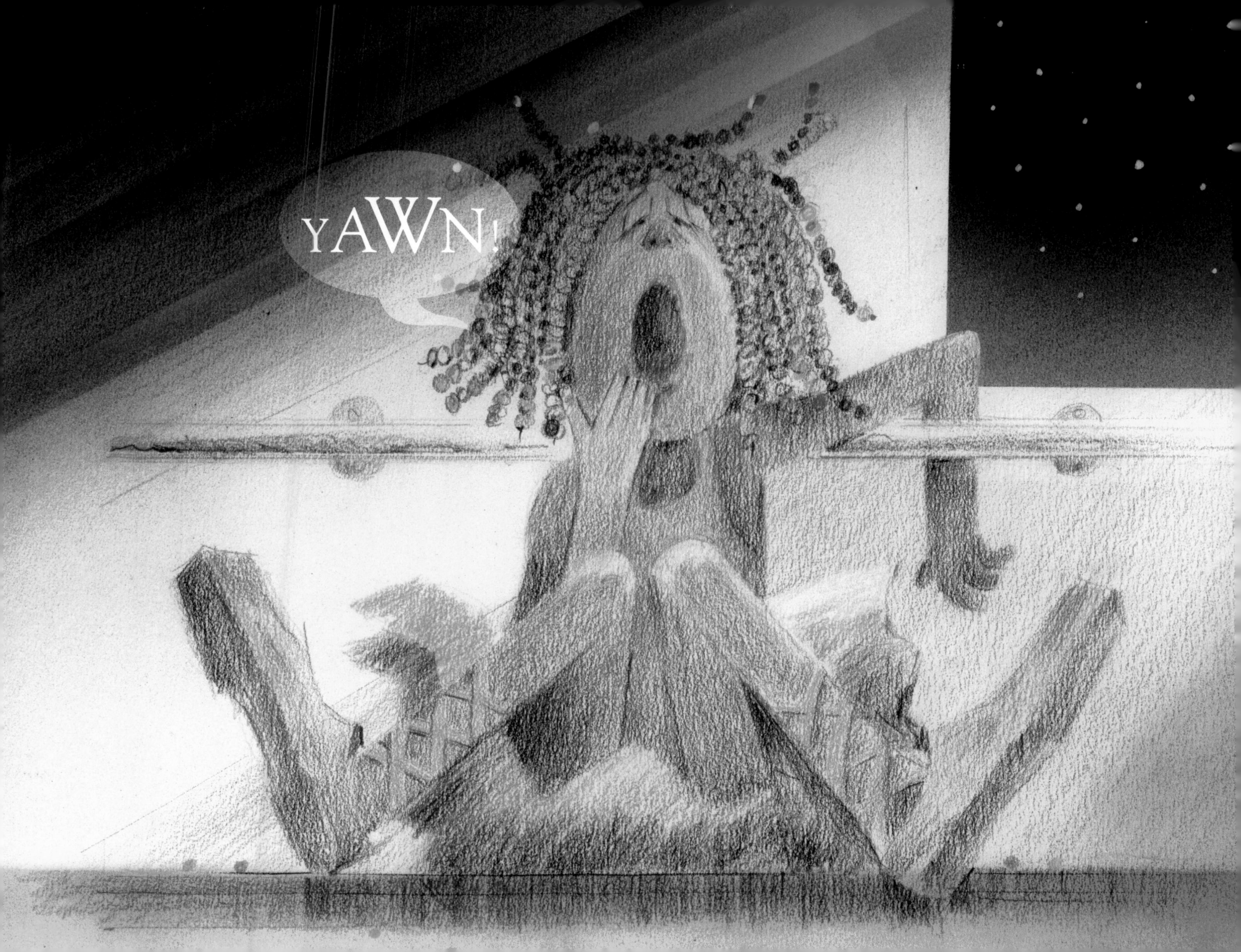
yAWN!

Chloe and Zoey and Lola...

Lucas,

and Lou.

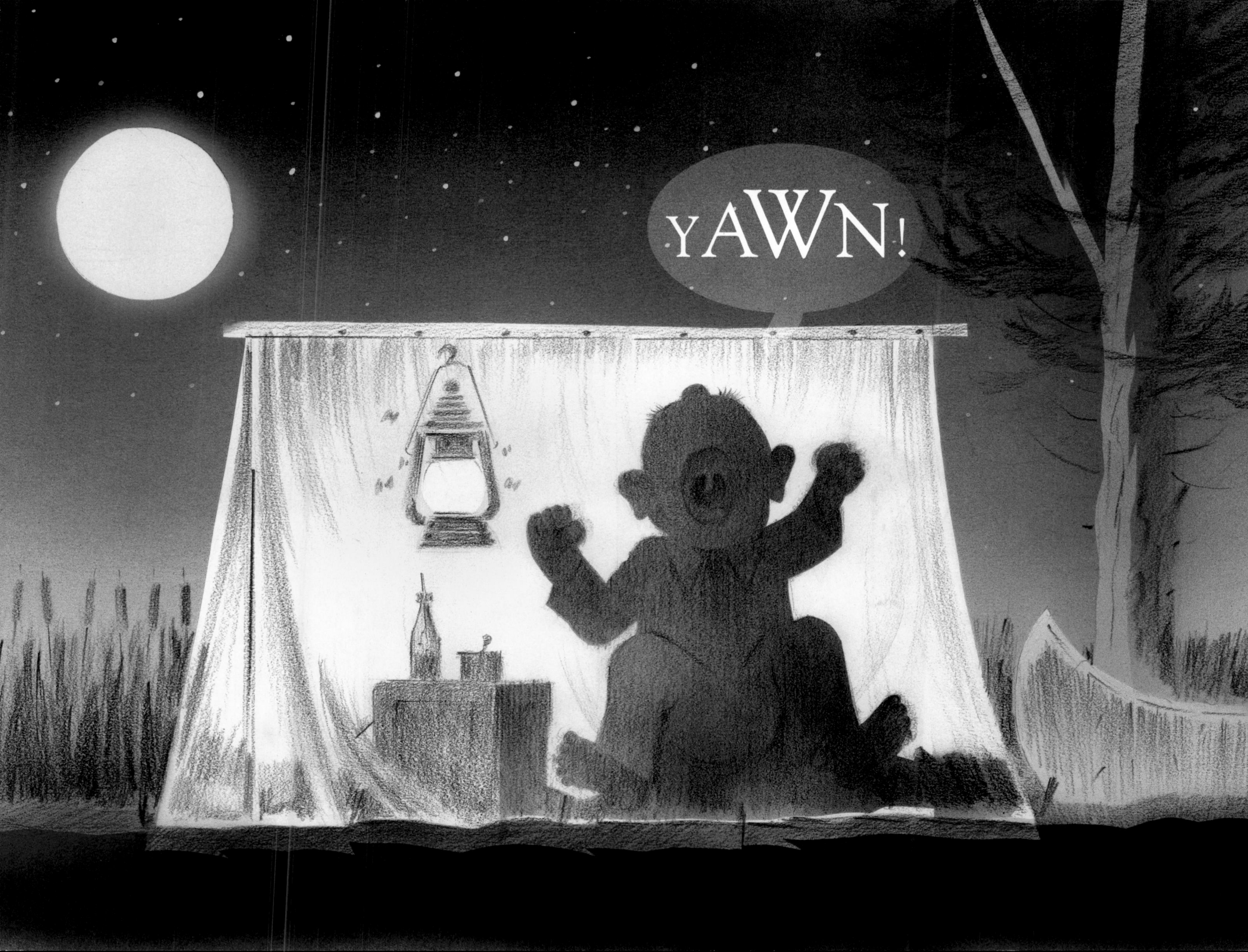
yAWN!

It's here, it's there...

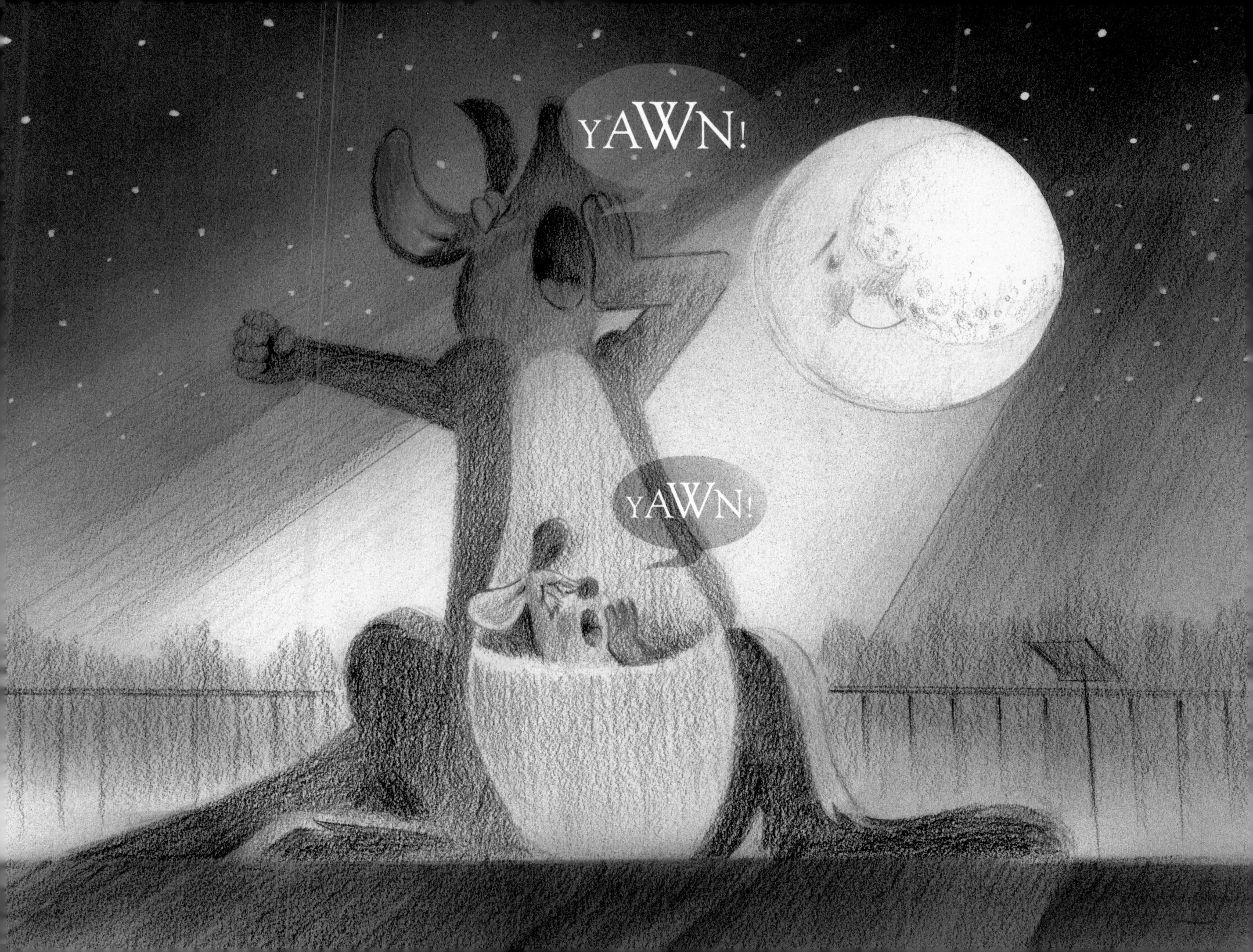
yAWN!
yAWN!

it's everywhere...

it's even at the zoo!

(Feel free to yawn now.)

On it goes to Carlos...

to Keona...

and Jin and Jang,

to every boy and girl.

Goodness gracious!

It's contagious!

This could go

’round the world!

Now the night is silent,

nagging troubles are all gone.

Now the world is peaceful,

and it started with a yawn.